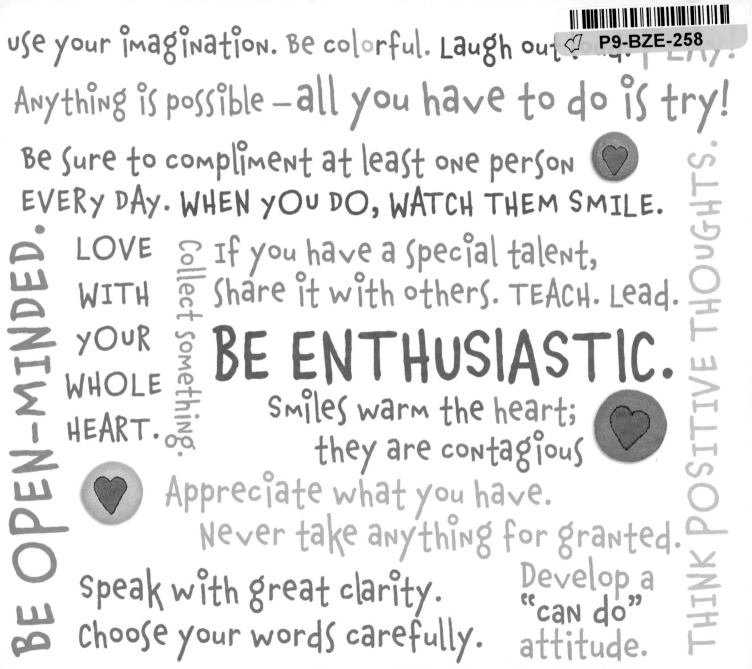

use your imagination. Be colorful. Laugh out loud. PLAY.

Anything is possible – all you have to do is try!

Be sure to compliment at least one person EVERY DAY. WHEN YOU DO, WATCH THEM SMILE.

BE OPEN-MINDED.

LOVE WITH YOUR WHOLE HEART.

Collect something.

If you have a special talent, share it with others. TEACH. Lead.

BE ENTHUSIASTIC.

Smiles warm the heart; they are contagious

Appreciate what you have. Never take anything for granted.

Speak with great clarity. Choose your words carefully.

Develop a "can do" attitude.

THINK POSITIVE THOUGHTS.

Only One You

by Linda Kranz

rising moon

www.risingmoonbooks.com

Composed in the United States of America

Edited by Theresa Howell
Designed by Katie Jennings
Photography by Klaus Kranz

FIRST IMPRESSION 2006
ISBN 10: 0-87358-901-7
ISBN 13: 978-0-87358-901-7

Printed in Mumbai, India October 2021

Library of Congress Cataloging-in-Publication Data Pending

Kranz, Linda,
Only one you / by Linda Kranz.
p. cm.
Summary: Adri promises to remember his parents' words of wisdom about how to live his life, such as
"Find your own way. you don't have to follow the crowd" and "Make wishes on the stars in the nighttime sky."
ISBN-13: 978-0-87358-901-7 (hardcover : alk. paper)
ISBN-10: 0-87358-901-7 (hardcover : alk. paper)
[1. Conduct of life--Fiction.] 1. Title.

P27.K8597laaw 2006
[E]--dc22

2006007550

For Klaus—I give you my  for safe keeping.

—L.K.

"It's time," Papa said.
"I think it is," Mama agreed.
"Time for what?" Adri asked.
Papa's voice softened,
"To share some wisdom."

Always be on the lookout

for a new friend.

Look for **beauty** wherever you are, and keep the memory of it with you.

Blend in when you need to.

Stand out when you have the chance.

Find your own way.
You don't have to follow the crowd.

know when
to SPEAK;
know when to

listen.

No matter how you look at it,

there is so much to discover.

If you make a wrong turn, circle back.

If something gets in your way,

move around it.

set aside
some quiet time
to relax and

reflect.

Every day.

Appreciate

art.

It's all around you!

make wishes on the stars
in the nighttime sky.

"Thank you for listening," Mama said. "We hope you will remember."
Papa winked and whispered, "We know this is a lot for you to think about."
Adri did a backwards somersault and smiled.
He was excited to go out into the world with what he had just learned.
"Wait for me!" he shouted to his friends.

Before he swam away,
he turned back to his parents and said,
"I will remember."
Mama kissed Adri on the top of his head.
"There's only one you in this great big world," she said.

"make it a better place."

Enjoy Look for the good in everyone. FIND
the
simple Breathe. Be good BALANCE.
things to yourself. Savor the
in life. good times.

Look for rainbows after a rain shower.

Be kind.

Do something nice
for someone.
They will remember
your kindness.

Take care of
YOU.

BE SPONTANEOUS

Choose friends that energize you
to feel good about yourself.

Life is a circle; enjoy the journey.

Speak your mind—gently.

When you feel joy, tell someone. Share your happiness.

FIND YOUR PASSION. You are AMAZING!

When things get hectic, Set goals, and go after them.
focus on being calm. Once you've accomplished
them—set new goals.

DREAM BIG!

Look for opportunities to excel.